This book belongs to:

Ellie

Disney FROZEN II

Spirits of Nature

Written by
NATASHA BOUCHARD

Illustrated by
THE DISNEY STORYBOOK ART TEAM

There were once four spirits of nature.
The spirits have not been seen for many years.

Elsa's power is growing. She blasts her magic. It wakes the spirits!

The trolls tell Elsa the spirits are upset.

Elsa must face the spirits. She will go to the Enchanted Forest.

Anna and Elsa go north.
Their friends go, too.

They find the Enchanted Forest behind a wall of mist.
The four spirits are wind, fire, water, and earth.

The Wind Spirit
is playful and friendly.

The Fire Spirit is
small but mighty.

The Wind Spirit swirls around the friends.
They fly into the air!

The Fire Spirit runs through the forest.
Elsa chases its fire with her ice power.

The Earth Giants are big
and powerful.

The Water Spirit
is swift,
like a horse.

The Earth Giants sleep by the river.
Anna and Olaf float by.
They stay very quiet.

The Water Spirit swims in the Dark Sea.
Elsa meets the Water Spirit.

Elsa faced the spirits! There will be peace throughout the land.